IUIIΨ

The Autistic Turtle

By

Thomas Morrow

Illustrated

By

Martha Evans

For Dad, Mom, Charlie and Abe

I love you!

Also dedicated to

CANDY

My very first turtle

CHAPTER ONE
Loud Noises!

One summer day, a turtle named Henry, was walking through the woods. Henry was an autistic turtle. I bet you wonder what an autistic turtle is!

Let me tell you.

Henry heard a noise in the woods one day. A man named Joe was cutting down a tree. His son Thomas, said "Hey, Dad, why do you need that wood?"

"We need to build a fire at the farm to keep us warm," said his Dad.

Thomas said, "Oh yeah! We're going to the farm this weekend. I can't wait! Dad, look! There's a turtle! Can we take him home?"

Dad said, "Let's leave him there because it will be getting colder soon, and he will need a place to hibernate for the winter."

Henry the Turtle saw Joe pick up the chain saw and thought, "I've got to get out of here! I've got to run to my home because cutting down a tree might be loud!" Henry *DID NOT* LIKE LOUD NOISES!

As Henry was running home, he saw his turtle friends. Their names were Hannah, Adam, Nicholas, Cristina, Cal and Luke. When he got home, he yelled, "HEY GUYS! Guess what I heard? Someone named Joe and his son, Thomas, were in the woods cutting down a tree."

His friends gathered around him and Luke said, "We know! We were watching. It was so cool! IT WAS SO LOUD!"

Henry said, "IT WAS NOT COOL! I DON'T LIKE LOUD NOISES FOR THE ONE HUNDREDTH TIME! I have autism!!!"

Then Henry said, "*Shhhhhhh*. Listen! What's that?"

"What's what?" said Luke.

"That!" said Henry.

"What's what?" said Nicholas.

"*THAT!*" said Henry.

"WHAT'S *WHAAAAATTTT?*" yelled Cristina.

"Don't you guys hear that? It's a mosquito breathing!" said Henry.

"We don't hear anything!" they all said together.

"Are you kidding? You guys can't hear that?" yelled Henry.

Hannah said, "It's because Henry is an autistic turtle. He hears things that we don't hear or pay attention to."

"Like what?" Cal asked.

Henry said, "Hear that? Butterfly wings. Hear that? Grass blades swishing. Hear that? Lady bug flying. Hear that? Moles digging deep underground."

"WOW!" said Cal "You hear all of that?"

"Yes," said Henry, "and all at the same time so it makes it hard for me to hear what Mrs. Bady, my teacher, or my mom and dad are saying. I can't even listen to everything you guys are saying because I am hearing all that other stuff."

"So you have super power hearing?" asked Luke.

Henry laughed. "I have super powers alright. I think my autism helps me focus on noises that are all around us every day, but you guys never notice. It's a gift really. Like I can tell my dad that something is about to break down because I notice it squeaking when no one else does! It comes in handy, but it can also keep me from hearing other stuff like my mom screaming, 'Henry, I have told you *three* times to come to dinner!"'"

Henry thought to himself, "Who can think of dinner when that swish, ping, ping, swish, ping, ping means our wind conditioner might be broken!"

"We are having your favorite! We're having worms and they are Night Crawlers!" said mom.

The wind conditioner was going to have to wait. "Night Crawlers! *Mmmmmm.* My favorite!" said Henry.

Chapter Two
Sensory

It was time for school and all young turtles had to go. The school was in Woodsville, which was in the middle of the woods. The clock on the wall chimed, (*Westminster chimes*) "Dong, dong, dong, dong, dong, dong, dong, dong." It was time for class to start. Everyone was in class. Let's see, there was Ben, Luke, Thomas, Henry D., Lucy, Jake, Maleah, Keeley, Cameron, Blake, Grant, Kelsey, Cooper, Sydney, Caleb, Gage, Vika, Nicholas, Tori, Jack, and me of course, Henry M.

Everyone was talking quietly at their desks. The desk tops were made out of bark from leftover trees that had been cut down. The rest of the desks were made by old turtles. They carved each one with rocks and sticks.

Mrs. Bady said, "Class, let's go to the moss for our morning meeting."

Thomas said, "Henry, why did you bring toys to the moss?"

Henry said, "They are fidgets! It is sensory."

Blake asked, "What is *sensory*?"

Then Luke said, "I don't know…what *IS* sensory?"

Jake, Cooper, Henry D. and Ben said at the same time, "Yeah, what *IS* sensory?"

"Well," Mrs. Bady said, "do you remember when we studied the five senses?"

The class said altogether, "Yes!"

"What are the five senses?" asked Mrs. Bady.

Sidney said, "Eyes!"

Nicholas yelled, "Touch!"

Tori said, "Hearing!"

"Taste!" said Cooper.

Meliah said, "Smell!"

Mrs. Bady said, "That is correct. Good job, class. There are some people that need to use their senses more and some people that need to use them less. You can't control how much sensory you are born with because God made you perfect just the way you are. Henry needs more sensory, like stuff that moves and stuff that is squishy. It feels good to Henry to have lots of pressure on his arms, legs, body, claws, toes, head, and, of course, on his shell and scales. When Henry wiggles on the moss or his toadstool, which looks like a human's Hokkie stool, it helps him concentrate. Wiggling just makes him feel better."

Henry M. raised his claw.

"Yes Henry," said Mrs. Bady, "What is your question?"

"When I was little, my mom and Mamaw used to play a game called 'He's Mine', all the time. (By the way, the name Mamaw is short for Grandma. I usually spell it Momo because that's how it *sounds* to me, but the Internet says it is spelled Mamaw.) Anyway, I would lay on the floor, and Mom would hold my feet and Mamaw would hold my arms. Mom would pull real hard and say, 'He's mine!' Then Mamaw would pull me back and say, 'No, he's mine.' Then Mom would pull me back again and say, 'NO! He's *mine*!' They stretched me out and it felt *sooooo* good!"

Mrs. Bady smiled and said, "And that's why Henry has toys on his desk. They are not really *toys*. They are sensory fidgets."

The whole class said at once, "*Ohhhhhhhhhhhhhhhhhhhhhhhhh!* Now we understand!"

Chapter Three
Bed Time

It was 6:30 pm and Henry was watching Turtle Tube videos. "What kind of videos do you asked?" *Stampy Cat*!

Henry said, "Only two more hours before I go to bed." He thought, "*NOOOOOOOOOOOOOOOOOOOOOOOOO*! I don't want to go to bed!"

Two hours later, Henry was in bed. *Four* hours later Henry was *still* awake and said, "I can't fall asleep. *Whyyyyyyyyyyyyyyyyy*?"

Henry thought for a minute. "Oh! Now I know. I forgot to take my super-duper Sleepy Medicine."

Henry had a very hard time going to sleep at night. A *VERY* hard time! He would think and think and think about everything that happened at school that day, and the day before and the day before that. He would think about all of his turtle friends, his birthday party next year, the pizza he had last week, Christmastime, *Stampylongnose*, and sometimes a spelling word would pop into his head. He thought, "*Really*? I can't even stop thinking about *spelling words*?????????????"

Henry needed to talk a lot before he could go to sleep. He needed to talk about 5 or 4 things. That would get his talking all out. Also, Henry needed to watch TV/S.M.B. which stands for *Stampy's Channel* on Turtle Tube. The "S" stands for *Stampy Cat*. The "M" stands for *Mine Craft*, the game *Stampy* plays. The "B" stands for *Barnaby*, his wolf, who follows him around in *Stampy's Lovely World*. Watching Turtle Tube made his eyes want to shut, and in two or three minutes, he was asleep.

Before Henry fell asleep, he would hear a sound like, "*Sha-sha, Sha-sha.*" It was the sound of the beads in his weighted blanket.

A weighted blanket gave him pressure so he wouldn't move. This helped him go to sleep.

P.S. Henry really loved to talk. He was lucky. Some turtles with autism can't talk.

Stampylongnose: You Tube,
https://www.youtube.com/user/stampylonghead

Chapter Four
Pain

One day, Henry went to play with his friends, Luke, Nicholas, Vika and Caleb. They were playing on a fort that was one foot high. Suddenly, Henry slipped and fell. His shell wasn't as strong as an adult's shell. His friends gasped! They tried to catch him, but it was no use. He had already hit the ground. Hard!

His friends asked, "Are you okay??? That must have really hurt!"

Luke said, "When I fell down like that once, it felt like I hit pointy rocks! It really hurt!"

Then Henry said, "I barely felt anything."

Everybody said, "*WHHAAAATTT*?"

Caleb said, "How is that possible?"

Henry said, "Remember how I told some of you that I have autism?"

Caleb and Nick said, "NO! You didn't tell us that. We must have been away, taking care of the pet lizards. We did not hear you say that you have autism."

Thomas rushed over because he heard what they were talking about. He said, "When I was little, my mom and dad thought that I had autism, but I didn't. It was a false alarm. I wish I did because Henry has super powers that I don't have."

Henry said, "Yah, like Turtle Power!"

"Hey! Let's get back to the story!" said Caleb.

Henry said, "Well, I feel stuff, but I don't feel stuff like you do. I have to be careful so I don't get hurt."

Thomas said, "Did you guys know that my mamaw and I are writing a book about an autistic turtle? We should put this information in our book!"

They all agreed that this was important information. All of Henry's friends said that they would protect him so he didn't get hurt.

Chapter Five
Family

One day, in winter, Henry was fighting with his brother, Charlie. Henry got a new game called *Terraria*. His brother wanted to play it, but Henry wanted to play by himself for a few minutes. (It's important for autistic turtles to have some time to themselves to stay calm.) Well, Charlie wanted to hog the game and play by himself for *two whole days*!

Henry said, "Charlie, it's not your game. I can use it whenever I want, and I don't have to share it!"

Then Charlie got mad. His eyebrows came together in a mean look. Charlie came after Henry, and Henry started after Charlie. Let me tell you…it wasn't pretty.

They started tackling each other. They were rolling around on the floor but not like in an "I love you" way. This was war.

Of course Henry shouldn't have said something so selfish, and Charlie shouldn't have *bitten* Henry. Their mom and dad came in to break up the fight and sent both Henry and Charlie to their rooms to "think about their actions."

Henry slammed his door. Charlie slammed *his* door. Henry threw some things around his room. He was really mad. He looked into his water turtle tank. Then he looked outside. He dug through his closet for something to do. After a little while, Henry started to calm down and remember the tools his therapists gave him to use when he got mad. He also remembered that he was learning to think about other people's feelings. That is something hard for autistic turtles to do.

Mom yelled from the bottom of the stairs, "Are you boys ready to do the right thing?"

Charlie yelled back, "I'm ready."

Henry yelled back, "I'm ready."

Mom said, "Then come down here! Henry, what did *you* do?"

Henry hung his head and said, "I should have thought about Charlie's feelings."

"That's right," said Mom, "and Charlie what did *you* do?"

"I shouldn't have...bitten...Henry in...the arm???" asked Charlie, trying to remember why he was sent to his room.

Ugh! Charlie never remembered what he did wrong!!!

"Yes, that's right," said Mom, "and now you two give each other a big hug and say you are sorry."

21

Henry and Charlie hugged each other and said, "I'm sorry." Henry *was* really sorry. He was learning so much about how other people feel and how he needed to think about others. He really loved his little brother, and Charlie always made him laugh with his silly jokes and the things he said. Charlie was thinking also. He was really sorry *too*. He had the best big brother ever, and he wanted to grow up and be just like Henry!

Another member of the family was Abe, the big white Great Pyrenees dog that weighed 150 pounds. Abe didn't know he was a dog and didn't know he was so big. When any of the mamaws or papaws came over, he would leap around and wag his tail. Usually, Charlie would go flying across the room with one wag of Abe's tail. Everyone would yell, "Abe, CLIMB!" That was his command to calm down and lay down.

Abe was *very* important to Henry. It was like he understood autism and would come running when Henry needed him. After school each day, if Henry laid on the floor, all 150 pounds of Abe would lay on top of him!

Henry would say, "Abe, get off of me!" Henry really didn't mind though. You would think it was bad that big Abe laid on top of him, but Abe's weight felt so good to Henry. Remember…sensory!

Sometimes Abe would kind of squish his teeth down on Henry's arm but not actually bite him. He would just put *pressure* on Henry's arms, and that felt really good too. Of course, there was lots of slobber, but Henry didn't mind.

When Henry would get upset or anxious or mad and would need to go to his room, Abe would run ahead and was always waiting for him. Henry would bury his head in Abe's thick, white fur. Pretty soon, he wasn't so upset.

A dog trainer came to the house one day. She said, "Abe is a natural therapy dog and your family is lucky to have him." He was raised in their home from a pup and Abe seemed to know Henry better than Henry knew himself. Henry and Abe were the very best of friends.

Henry's parents were really great. They did not stick their heads in their shell when they thought that Henry *might* have autism. Before he was even diagnosed at the age of three, Henry's parents got lots of information, attended classes, read books and got special doctors and therapists to help him be all that God made him to be.

Henry's parents loved him and Charlie more than anything in the world.

Chapter Six
Holidays and Parties

Halloween

Henry loved holidays! It didn't matter what holiday it was. He just loved holidays! One day in July he said, "Mom, I can't wait for Halloween this year. I want to start thinking about Halloween and what I would like to be for trick-or-treating."

Henry's mom said, "It's only July! We have three months before Halloween. That is a long time to think about something."

Thinking about something wasn't hard for Henry. He would think about something all the time until he couldn't think of *anything* else. Sometimes, turtles with autism have only one thing in their head, and there is not room to think about any other things. When he thought about something, he wanted to *talk* about it *all the time*. Like what he wanted to be for Halloween.

Sometimes Henry's mom would say that he could only talk about whatever he was thinking for ten minutes, and then he would have to stop talking about it for ten more minutes. It was *so* hard for Henry *not* to talk about what was in his head for ten minutes!

CHRISTMAS

Christmas was Henry's favorite holiday. He would help his dad put up Christmas lights outside and help his mom put up the *BIG* Christmas tree, plus four other Christmas trees they had in their house. Henry and Charlie even had a Christmas tree in each of their bedrooms!

When it was time to put up the big Christmas tree, with hundreds of ornaments, he knew exactly where every ornament should go from the year before. He would say, "Mom, that doesn't go there. That ornament goes right here!"

It was like he had a picture of the tree in his head and remembered where every ornament went.

There was just one thing about holidays and parties. Autistic turtles get so excited, nervous and anxious about holidays and parties that it makes these times very hard to get through. Remember, autistic turtles

29

see and hear things that regular turtles do not. So holidays and parties, with all the decorations, sounds and people, have a lot more going on than most turtles realize.

Henry had a lot of parties to go to during the Christmas holidays. He had Christmas breakfast with Mamaw Jane, Papaw Jack (who was really Papaw Paul), Aunt Kathy and Uncle Dan. His cousins, Sam and George, were also there. That was fun.

Then he had Christmas dinner with Grandma Bean (who was really Grandma Kathy), and Papaw Forklift, (who was really Papaw Web), and more cousins. That was fun.

He had Christmas lunch with Papaw Tom, Grandma Lisa, Ellie, Colson, Aunt Mary and lots of other people. That was fun.

He had another Christmas breakfast with Mamaw Baking (who was really Mamaw B), and Papaw Money (who was really Papaw B. He was Papaw Money because he always had quarters for the claw machine.) Aunt Dana and Cousin Mackenzie were there too, and that was fun!

He had Christmas Eve dinner with Aunt Cindy, Uncle Michael, and another cousin, Cassie Paige. Aunt Dana and Mackenzie where there too. Then he had Christmas night back at Mamaw Jane and Papaw Paul's house.

All that "fun" was beginning to wear Henry out!

His favorite was the day he celebrated Christmas with just his mom, dad and little brother, Charlie. Everything was calm and quiet except for Henry and Charlie yelling every time they opened a present. He got to stay in his pajamas all day long and do *nothing* but play!

Henry worried about a lot of stuff around the holidays. They were kind of a stressful time for him.

He would think, "I wonder what happens when the Elf on the Shelf stops pranking us and goes away?"

He would worry about what he wanted for Christmas and what he might not get.

At all the parties there was lots of noise and lights and sometimes people he didn't know. He didn't like people *he didn't know*. Autistic turtles don't like people they don't know because the people are *new*.

Henry would think, "I don't like these new people because *I don't like change*, and these people weren't here last year. *Grrrrrr.* Why do things have to change? I DON'T LIKE CHANGE!"

Henry's mind was so full of stuff he thought to himself, "I think my head might pop off."

Henry's parents were very smart. They had secret codes for when Henry had just had *too much* of all the people, noise, lights, food and craziness. Henry would squeeze his dad's claw and that was the code for, "I HAVE HAD ENOUGH!!!"

Then Henry's dad would stop whatever he was doing and say, "Do you need a break, Buddy?"

He would take Henry to a quiet place or for a long walk, even in the snow, rain and cold, so that he could have quiet. By learning when he had *too much* of all the good things about holidays, Henry could take breaks that helped him get through and even learned to enjoy them.

Birthdays

It was June 28th and a nice summer day. It was Henry's birthday. After he opened all of his stuff, like *Terraria* and *Mine Craft*, he went to play with his new games. Then he remembered a bad experience he had. He was at a restaurant called the "Red Rooster" once with his family. The waiters came to sing, "Happy, Happy Birthday" to someone at another table. It was loud singing, and they were clapping. Henry got so upset that he threw a kids' menu at the table having the birthday party, but he missed. He didn't like the party because it was someone *else's* party.

Autistic turtles have to learn to share and have fun at other peoples' birthdays. Mostly, just *other* peoples' birthdays. He didn't mind his friends' and family members' birthdays.

The lady that Henry threw the menu at came to talk to his family. She wasn't mad and even told his parents that he had a good throwing arm. Henry didn't mean to hit the lady. He just missed his target and the flying menu fell into her lap! He learned that it is not correct to throw things in a restaurant, no matter how angry you get.

As Henry got older, he liked birthdays about three percent more than he used to. Henry hollered at his mom one day and said, "Hey, Mom! I'm at three percent now."

His mom asked, "three percent of what?"

"I like birthday parties three percent more than I used to!!!"

Henry was improving and getting used to new things so fast. He actually planned and helped decorate for baby Angela's one-year-old birthday party at church. Angela's parents, Adelso and Lupe thought that the decorations were very pretty. They were surprised that Henry had helped. Henry liked helping with Angela's birthday party. He had a really good time.

Chapter Seven
Review and Suggestions

Let's review some things you should know about autistic turtles and some other suggestions.

Autistic turtles:

- They don't like loud noises, but they may be very noisy themselves. Loud noises may hurt their ears.
- They hear and see things that regular turtles don't. In a quiet classroom, they will still hear many sounds that are distracting. In a noisy classroom, forget it. No concentration!
- Since they hear and see things that others don't, it can be a really good thing. They see and hear the world differently and can see even the smallest things that God has created.
- They like worms!

- They have different levels of sensory needs. They may need more sensory or less. They may need to chew on an eraser at the end of a pencil or fidget with something in their hands so that they can concentrate. It can be hard to keep their feet and body in one place, so wiggling is important to their learning. Just let them wiggle and move!
- They may need lots of pressure on different parts of their body to help them be calm and relaxed. But some turtles with autism don't want any pressure on their body. Even light pressure can be painful. They have to learn what helps them to be calm.
- They may have a hard time falling asleep because so much thinking is going on in their head.
- They may need a strict routine, doing exactly the same thing every night, in order to go to sleep. Watching a video or listening to the same music or sounds every night could really help.

- They don't always feel pain or may feel pain more intensely. Those that don't feel pain the way others do can be in danger because they can get hurt without even realizing it.
- They have to learn about the feelings of others, and *someone* has to teach them.
- They need quiet time alone sometimes. They might need just a few minutes or sometimes much longer.
- They may need an animal companion. Animals can be very helpful. Therapy dogs are the best.
- They need the support of parents, family, churches and teachers. The supporters need to learn *everything they can* about autism. According to the Center for Disease Control (CDC), February 2015, humans have autism too! One out of 68 children have autism. One out of 42 boys and 1 out of 189 girl have autism, and it may not be diagnosed. Is your child autistic?

- They may feel that holidays and parties can be the most fun but also the most stressful times. Everyone should have a safe, quiet place to go to get away from all the noise and people for a little while. Parents need to get that!
- They need very strict routines to follow.
- They do not like change. They have plans in their mind for how things should go and when that is changed, it is very stressful and upsetting. Tell them the new plan. Let them have time to adjust to the new plan! Change is very hard and unsettling. Routine is good…change, not so much.
- Their grandparents, aunts, and uncles should understand autism! Go to the World Wide Web and learn about it.
- Their food should not contain Red 40 dye food additives. Food dye is bad. Red 40 food dye is *really* bad!
- They can't always say why something bothers them because they can't put it

into words. Just listen and help them grow through it.
- Lots of people have a part to play in making an autistic turtle successful.

Chapter Eight
The Real Story...
Behind the Story

So now you know more about how autistic turtles think and feel. I guess by now you have figured out that this story is not really about a turtle named Henry, but it's about my own story!

I really wanted my classmates to understand why I have toys that are really fidgets on my desk and lots of other things about autism. I wanted to help other people who might have autism but might not know it. My classmates are the best. We help each other learn, and they are always there to help me. And I'm there to help them too.

My teacher, Mrs. Bady, is an awesome teacher. She helps me and encourages me to be the very best *me* I can be! My resource teacher, Mrs. Smith; music teacher, Mrs.

Peters; and art teacher, Mrs. Hannon; (I love art!), are also there to help me and they are awesome teachers too.

My principal, Mrs. Dolak, has made our school one of the very best in the United States. She accepts all kids just the way God made them. My assistant principal, Mrs. B., is awesome too. Mrs. B was my first grade teacher and she helped me *so* much. Everyone at my school is really nice. Ms. CeeCee, who works in the office, is especially nice. Mr. Williams, who does *everything* around my school, is really nice too!

My family, church, school, teachers, friends, therapists and doctors have all helped me along the way, and I am very thankful. I'm just a regular second grade kid that does regular second grade kid stuff and my autism is part of what makes me…well…ME!

Thanks for reading *The Autistic Turtle*! I hope you have learned something about autism.

THE END

Resources

Autism Speaks:

www.autismspeaks.org

Behavior Solutions: Dr. Colin M. Peeler, BCBA-D, LBA

http://www.behsolutions.com/index.htm

Mercy Autism Center: Early Childhood

http://www.mercy.net/practice/mercy-autism-center

Dr. John F. Mantovani, M.D. - Neurologist

http://www.mercy.net/practice/mercy-clinic-child-neurology-0

Mercy Clinic Child Neurology:

http://www.mercy.net/practice/mercy-clinic-child-neurology-0

Dr. Lynda Brady, M.D. - Pediatric Gastroenterologist:

http://www.mercy.net/node/11198

Dr. Dan Wentz, D.V.M. - Veterinarian and Turtle specialist

www.fergusonanimal.com

Mrs. Martha Evans – Illustrations

martgraphics@yahoo.com

Hokkie Chair:

http://www.amazon.com

Cozy Swing: Lori Hammock Swing

www.autism-products.com

Fidgets:

www.discountschoolsupply.com

www.autism-products.com

Weighted Blanket:

www.autism-products.com

Stampy Cat, Stampy's Lovely World, Barnaby:

https://www.youtube.com/user/stampylonghead

The Tree House Learning Center:

www.thetreehouselearningcenter.com

Andreas Gluten-Free: The best gluten free food sold!

www.andreasglutenfree.com

If you would like to learn more, go to: www.autisticturtle.com – Coming soon…

If you would like to get a copy of, *The Autistic Turtle*, contact the director of marketing, Mamaw Jane. Just leave your name and number and she will call you back! Call 314-570-6691 or email to bickhamjf@centurytel.net.

About the author…

Thomas lives with his mom, dad, little brother, Charlie, and big white Pyrenees dog, Abe. He is the president of his company, *Turtle Protectors*, which is made up of adults and children who are committed to rescuing abandoned or injured turtles. He and his brother currently have 30 land and water turtles and one tortoise. With their father, Thomas and Charlie, have helped to build extensive turtle habitats inside their home and in their yard.

Thomas enjoys time away at the farm and riding four wheelers, dirt bikes, go carts and basically, anything that is fast and furious. He takes skateboard lessons and loves to play video games. He especially likes the *Stampy Cat* and *Sky Lander Family* video channels. He attends baseball camp in the summer and has played on a soccer team. Thomas really likes music and art. He loves to swim and he is very good at basketball.

Update August, 2015: Thomas wrote this book from February to May, 2015 while he was eight years old. He has just turned nine, started third grade and lost a tooth during his first week of school! He *really* likes his new teacher, Miss Hoffman.